Paradise, Sunset
By Tho

Contents

Contents	2
Contents	4
Paradise, and the cold dark	6
The barren lands.	8
Ruins	10
The dance of a blade.	11
The elegance of nothingness.	12
Autumn leaves.	13
A rose by any other name…	14
The beauty of a heartbeat.	16
War.	17
Under the starlight.	18
Like clockwork.	19
The Flames of fluidity.	20
Anxious silence.	21
Mists of the sunlight.	23
The planet cracker	24
Colour	26
Waiting for the light in your eyes.	28
The Leviathan.	30
Light speed.	33
Chased.	41
A simple kiss.	42
Conformity.	43

Artificial	47
Lonely road	49
The waterfall.	50
They Cackle.	51
Pebbles.	52
Only human.	54
Precious.	57
Children.	58
A shield from the nightmares.	60
The field of dreams.	61
The island.	62
The blast wave.	63
Benevolence.	65
Guardian.	67
The storm.	68
Detention.	69
Solitude.	70
A blade in a ballet.	71
The crystal kingdom.	73
From dusk to dawn.	74
The blank canvas.	75
Embers.	76
Once…	77
Such empty tears.	78
A rose in a blizzard.	79
Interlinked.	80
Alone in death…	81
A machine.	82

Wouldn't you rather? 83

Through the eyes of a trinket. 84

The northern lights. 87

Doves. 88

Shriek. 89

Paradise, Sunset and Nothingness. 92

For Emma

Paradise, and the cold dark

She clumsily rose to her feet, the scent of roses surrounding her, enticing her with sweetness. This garden of Eden was no paradise; there was only darkness, the illusion of light was fading, and with it, she too would simply wither away.

The woman's head throbbed, pain pulsing and pulsing with no foreseeable end, with no limit. Cherry blossom drifted around her, whispering in hushed voices, 'follow,' 'follow'… Beautiful light shone down upon emerald blades of grass, reflecting elegantly - its light. Blinding yet radiant, and beautiful. White clouds floated along the ocean - the blue stream that was the sky, a sea of perfect sapphire that stretched as far as the eye could see. Soon this would all crumble to dust in the wake of the end, and after that, only darkness could follow. The woman turned to face the lone cherry blossom tree in this field of paradise, and she smiled lightly.

"Thy end, is nigh."

~

He woke with a start, the dream of falling fresh in his mind. Cold and darkness attacked him as his eyes darted, desperately searching for light. Drip. Drip. Water fell with an unfamiliar softness as it splashed against stone, the sound bouncing across the cavern of nothingness, echoing through shadows. A damp, sinister wind swept through the cavern, calling, shouting, barking, 'Run', 'Run!'. There must be light, he knew, and he knew that in the darkest of places, in the blackest of nights, the light only shone brightest.

His head throbbed as he scampered to his feet; his movements were quick, undisciplined, fearful. Only darkness existed in this land of chaos, only darkness… But then, a spot of light. Another. Another. This world of darkness was crumbling, the absolute reality that all was darkness, was changing, and soon it would be no more, and with it, well, a creature of darkness held no place in the light.

~

The edge of paradise was crumbling, and she could see the precipice of darkness growing ever closer, and with it, two blue eyes; however, they were neither evil nor menacing, was she not destined for death?

Visions of light smashed through the mouth of this hungry cavern, and with it, a beautiful creature became visible through his blank, empty eyes. Was he not destined for destruction?

The darkness conjoined with the light, it mixed, the light drove away the darkness, yet it fed it more power, it cast more shadows.

The woman stepped onto cold stone, a shiver travelled up her spine.

The man stepped onto emerald grass, the softness cushioned his bruised feet, as he protected his eyes from solar beauty.

"Hello?" He asked as he caught sight of her.

"Greetings, one of darkness." She flashed a smile, and added a curt bow. His blue eyes blinked at her smile, as her pink orbs stared back into his sapphire pools.

"My heart is but darkness, in a cage of black, but perhaps your white light is a key?"

"I am but a key without a lock, without purpose. Perhaps this is my purpose?"

The barren lands.

The sky cracked with thunder, grey clouds swirling above dark falling ash that scorched the air and land. Lightning flashed across the barren landscape, any memoir of verdant grass or sapphire was long since destroyed by the harsh heat that surrounded the desert plains. The menacing volcano miles ahead bellowed down upon the land, spitting its hell fire fury as it sat alone, high above the lands that surrounded it.

An earthquake left the land scarred, the jagged line cutting through the dead oak tree that now dangled over the chasm by its roots, desperate to be released, to stop struggling, to end its stubborn and lonely existence. Pit. Pat. Rain began to fall, the swirling mass of grey above spilling its contents onto the dead, dry land. The tiny splash of water on a grain of sand echoed across the barren plains, before the torrent of tears attacked the earth from the cracked sky.

Sandals crunched across ash and grainy sand, the sole form of life on this lonely plain, stumbling towards the menacing volcano. The bundle of cloth in her arms treasured the corrupting power in which she craved. She unwrapped it, staring into the red glow it emitted. The glass orb vibrated, her energy being siphoned from simply gazing upon it. She swiftly wrapped it once again, and continued her path toward the lonely mountain.

She stared down with wide eyes into the molten rock that spat and flared out of the bellowing volcano in which it resided.

"It wasn't worth it."

She pulled back her hood, revealed the black scarred skin, the veins that were an unhealthy shade of violet.

"I need this life no more."

She threw herself forward, and tumbled with the red orb into the hellish pool of molten rock.

The barren plains, the lonely, desert plains. The plains that she caused to exist. Her cracked sky. Her scarred land. Her tree. Its roots gave in with one final crack, and it fell into the chasm of darkness.

Ruins

I pushed some rubble out of the entrance, and drifted into the sandstone hall. Light filtered in through a hole in the ceiling, illuminating a hall of pillars. The third pillar on the left had been smashed, crumbled into blocks of stone and grains of sand that swept across the stone tiles beneath my feet. Beautiful sculpted statues gazed at me, their stone glares feeling as cold as the room I stood in, their cold staring forced a shiver down my spine, before I reminded myself that they were inanimate. These were the ancient statues of the old gods, of those gods that the ones before us worshipped. Those ancient few. I continued through the sandstone hall, a cracked and decrepit, yet beautiful and tranquil ruin. The blue sky above would soon tint orange with the rush of an approaching sandstorm, I had to be quick. I pushed onward.

At the end of the entrance hall, the building opened up to a darker room, lit only by the light that slipped through the cracks, In the centre, an altar, a blade sitting atop. I gripped its leathery handle with purpose and hoisted it into the air. Despite its age, its condition was immaculate, and its weight crushing. I turned, and ran out of the ruin, pulling down my goggles and pushing up my mask as the sandstorm passed over me, pelting me with the grains of rock, once again burying the ruin in history.

The dance of a blade.

It dashed forward, slashing through sapphire rain drops, splitting the tiny gems in two as it continued on its path. Red burst into the rain, the crimson mixing with the rain covering the sapphire in red, colouring gems in ruby. The ruby rain cracked on cold concrete, spilling the crimson innards on cold hard ground. It continued to travel through the rain, spinning in her hand, sapphire gems cleansed the blade of its ruby stains as it danced under the flashes of lightning, plunging into warm ruby as she thrust it into a flesh casing. It scraped past alabaster bone, broke through malleable liver. A shrill cry resonated above, a dull thud echoed throughout its body, the heartbeat that slowly came to a stop. She ripped it out, pulling ruby with it, once again mixing it with the sapphire rain.

She stood alone, the three men lay dead around her, the liquid ruby that poured from the wounds drifted across the concrete under the hail if the azure monsoon, a cold night that mixed with the warmth of death. Her dancing blade finished its piece, and fell to the ground, resonating as its steel vibrated. The ruby stained metal sat under the assault of sapphire rain, the liquid gems drifting into chains.

The ruby clung to her hands; however, this blood would not disappear.

The elegance of nothingness.

It was a beautiful, a still and tranquil scene. A scene that showcased true peace. No twinkling stars burned in the distance, no planets span as they orbited the heart of the non-existent system, all that was here, was nothing. Here none of the cruelties of the universe existed, none of the pain. None of the suffering, no fear, no anger. Here; emotion was an abstract concept, a simple principal, an idea. None of it existed, nothing existed, but it was oh so beautiful. It was elegant, the weight of emptiness, a void of allure that stretched out in all possible directions. Nothing existed, and yet all of it was graceful, a splendorous grandeur of bleak existence. Happiness, joy, they didn't exist either, they didn't pollute the artistry, of this pulchritudinous nothingness. The deepest black of the darkest night, black, a colour meaning devoid of colour, an emptiness, a shade of nothing, but a shade of glamour.

The void was gorgeous, a world of beautiful emptiness, even though nothing existed, it was everything he wanted. He closed his eyes, and fell into an endless slumber.

Autumn leaves.

The crinkle of dried leaves sounded throughout the footpath, as they drifted across the breeze like cherry blossom at the dawn of spring. Cool air floated through the trees, giving brown, green and yellow leaves a final push before they glided through the chilled air, hovering over fall's breeze, a cold movement of cycling air. The trees were preparing to hibernate through another winter, to bare their branches for the world to see. Squirrels were gathering their nuts, scampering across dried leaves with a satisfying crunch. Glowing clouds floated on above, reflecting the white glare of the fading sun, the scent of emerald grass swirling in the air.

Autumn, the black to spring's white, the fall of the year.

A rose by any other name...

The alarm rang at five am, blasting through the small room in which I reside. Dawn breaks outside the window, birds are chirping, leaves are falling. Autumn, countryside, I had hope for today. Today was a new day, and once again my hands were that of another person. This dreary room was not my own, the emptiness, the cold. The lack of decoration made me wonder what kind of person lived in this body before me, and would live in it once again after I left it.

Six years. Six years of waking up in another person's body, living another person's life. The amount of relationships I had ruined, the amount of wealth I had squandered, I felt sorry for those lives I had ruined, that I had left in my wake. My younger self had decided that since I was in another person's life, my actions would have no consequences on myself, I cared not for anyone of who's existence I wrecked. I was twenty-one now, I had developed my own morality, forced myself to empathise.

"Honey! Get up!" I heard shouting downstairs, family? Lover? Information. I needed it. The first noteworthy thing I discovered is that I was female, a rare occurrence but not one that I hadn't dealt with before. One thing that never changed was my age, I was twenty-one, and so was every single person that I possessed. I often wondered what happened to my own body, but that lead to a spiral of depression, a road that led me to end a life, a beating heart that I ended with my own hands. Once I realised that I would wake up in the morning anyway, death became futile.

"Charlie!"

I was running out of time, I had a name, an age and a gender. What was I? Rich? Poor? English. I knew English, that was important. I decided to get changed and made my way downstairs.

"Hi…" I said, cautiously.

"What's up? You seem down."

"Rough night I guess. I didn't sleep much." I hoped that was true.

"Hmm. You did seem a little fidgety." That seemed to indicate we slept together, a lover then?

"What are we doing today again?"

"Forgot already have we?" He chuckled, this was going pretty well, I could play this out.

A sweet aroma wafted through the kitchen, he was cooking something, an omelette. I didn't like omelettes in my last body, but every life was different, everyday a learning experience, before everything reset.

I didn't want this one to reset. This life seemed simply… Nice. Especially after the last one had ended in the middle of Afghanistan, fighting for my life with no military experience. Yes. I could get used to this… Before it all reset.

The beauty of a heartbeat.

An instant, a moment, a breath. A heart, this muscle, this red beast that forces the crimson liquid to rush around a mechanism of cells and chemistry. This single moment in which so much energy, so much power is supplied to a wondrous synchronisation of organic material. A heartbeat, also a word to describe a moment, a single flap of a butterfly's wings as it descends upon a pebble in a pool, a ripple across a still lake that reflected the solar rays drifting in-between the clouds, a single droplet bounding, mixing, and bouncing back out of the body in which it fell, before it is assimilated into the mass of liquid in which it joined.

A heartbeat, it fluttered and skipped as the mind above connected with another, their heartbeats fell into sync as their lips brushed against one another, a perfect harmonious connection of two souls, two heartbeats. The gliding leaves fell around them, a bird chirped above under the red of the sunset, its wings flapping to the beat of the hearts below.

Out there, a million miles away, atoms crashed and smashed in the space between that beating, powering a star, an incredible sphere of power, of alluring light. Down between atoms, in the space between particles, in another dimension, a race, a civilisation flourished under the sound of the heartbeat, unbeknownst to the beauty of the beating above.

Lup dup. Lup dup.

He smiled to himself, all that was happening, all from the muscle within his chest.

War.

Falling, deep into the abyss. The destruction of a planet, the massacre of its people. On the left, the memory of an ally, a woman burning with the light of a thousand suns, her radiance more powerful and beautiful than any star. Alabaster ash, foes that stood against such heat, such ferocity. Blessed wounds, cleansing fire, beauty in death. The vanity of war.

An industry, an economy. Sneering men with powerful grins, a toy, a reason, another path to profit. The loss of life was simply a distraction, a disguise for the profit they desired. Money, an aspect of war that powered an army. All for a cotton dollar, a piece of useless fabric. The vanity of war.

The cannon fodder, the infantry, the grunt. The one who risked his life for his country, the one who loved his home, the one who lost his everything. The sacrifices of the many to support those greedy few. The vanity, of war.

Under the starlight

A lone hill, basking in the cold darkness of the night. No buildings to steal the sky, no cars flying by to pollute the world with noise, just cold, and quiet. There were no chirping birds, no scampering squirrels. All that illuminated the lonely night was the brilliance that lay beyond the darkness of the sky. Shining, radiant stars danced across the bleak void above, glistening millions and billions of miles away. The swirling colourful clouds of star dust that lit up the night's sky, nebulae, beautiful purples and turquoise that flashed across nothingness, a mass of pulchritudinous waste that provided the most brilliant vibrancy for all to see. The moon that floated over the night sky seemed bigger and closer than ever before, bouncing the light from the glowing sun back to earth. A lone tree sat atop the hill, sat under the universe, alone - encased in shadow, but beautiful non the less. In the grand scheme of the universe, this moment was evanescent, a fleeting spectacle, but down there, this moment lasted for an eternity. When everything came together, to show true beauty.

Like clockwork.

Cogs jerked and halted as they turned and twisted around an axis, their golden bronze finish flashing under the hint of light that made it through the face of the clock. Hands turned step by step as the cogs manipulated the plastic limbs, the teller of time, the inner workings of an ingenious invention. Like clockwork, the perfect movements of the perfect system, a mechanical set of works that managed to change the world, a tiny system that when incorporated into industrial machinery created an age of advancement, the perfect system. The inter connection of sculpted cogs, pistons and steam blasting out of vents, a whistling creature. A golem, large and pretty, a beautiful golden clockwork guardian standing by the memories of a time gone by.

This dystopian world, clockwork was incredible to them, alien to them, but still wondrous, still full of splendour. He stood guard by the grave of his maker, the one who invented his clockwork, his mechanical mind replaying memories of those days left in the clutches of the past. This world was unstoppable, time a flowing river that could be held by no dam. A world of perfect inter working cogs, a system of synchronised movement.

Like clockwork.

The Flames of fluidity.

An element that blazed a path of destruction, that calm ripped through the landscape, leaving only grey ash in its wake. An emblem of burning determination, a symbol of ferocious rage, such pulchritudinous orange. It sprints across a line of fuel with the elegance of a gazelle, and the lethality of a lion. It illuminates the darkest of nights, flickering and giggling as it watched people dance around it. It shares its warmth, it breathes its life, whilst it waits to devour all that it touches; the great devourer: fire.

It swirls and turns and twists as it rushes down a river, crashing against rocks, eroding them, taking them with it on its path to the end. An unstoppable force that smashes through all that stand against it. It washes away scars, memories, a life in its rampant charge, its unstoppable rampage. It flows, gently twirling as it is poured from height, the great giver of life, the most essential resource on the planet. Rolling, frolicking, crashing waves and soft, calm, rippling tranquillity. The giver and taker of life: water.

The giver and the taker douses the great devourer, equal and opposite, stronger and yet weaker. The burning light fades to black, the swirling sapphire desiccates to bleakness.

Anxious silence.

Silence drifted around the room, trying to escape. It didn't want to be in here, these people were just so... Awkward. It floated by the walls, glided past the window. It wanted to scream, to shout, but it couldn't, it would contradict its very existence. She was silence, the sound of nothingness, a beacon of darkness, her presence kept them quiet, and their silence kept her present. Her cloak trailed behind her, shadows swirled at her feet, and covered her face. Her thin, bony fingers gave the appearance of death herself, but she was not so dark, not so prestigious, not so commanding. She just had to wait for them to speak, to break this awkward silence. She sighed in perfect quiet, and sat beside the two unknowing people, twiddling her thumbs in anxiety.

"Hola! Hello! My old friend!"

Thunder cracked outside, it made silence jump in fear, and she rushed to the corner to hide herself. Sound crashed in through the window, his immaterial form phasing through the glass. He stood with a huge grin.

The young woman, previously sitting in silence, yelled at the thunder, causing the man to chuckle and to comfort her. She could have left then, her job was complete, should sound stay. This was his area of expertise, after all.

"Don't go yet! You haven't said hi!" Sound chuckled. Silence pointed at her throat and shook her head. Mute. As was fitting for the being of silence.

"Ah! I'm sorry ma'am! I should have remembered, how long has it been?" Silence held up her index finger. One.

"One year? One year since we've been in the same room? Wow." He whistled. In everything he did, he made noise. Too much noise, too many sounds, so annoying. She just wanted to leave, to run and isolate herself, but she lingered a little longer, knowing that with the nature of sound, he was likely to leave at any moment. Without sound, silence had to remain. Without her there had to be sound, or nothingness.

"I'll linger, for once; if you wish you may take your leave."

Silence widened her eyes, before bowing in thanks and floating out of the vicinity, and into the dark.

A silent night followed, it was dark, cold, but held the warmth of a smile.

Mists of the sunlight.

A white layer of cold that covered the morning, a thick haze of heavy water, a silvery grey cloud that drifted across the ground. Morning dew dripped from leaves and blades of emerald grass. The crunch of twigs and scamper of squirrels woke the forest from its slumber, its creatures coming into the hazy morn. The canopy of verdant leaves as droplets of water floated around blooming flowers and anchoring roots.

The sun, in its magnificent radiance had broken dawn, and had started to shine down upon the forest as the fresh morning progressed through to noon. Beauty, was encapsulated. Rays of light broke the greenery, and lit up the mist with rays of thick sunlight, illuminated specs of shining vapour that made the sunlight look hardened, physical, twinkling like golden ropes firing into the forest. The emerald grass that rocked in the breeze lit with vigour, re-colouring the pulchritudinous forest.

The planet cracker

The sky shook with terror as pure, evil power ripped across the atmosphere. Pure kinetic energy mixed with photons of light poured onto the surface at a speed of which the people were incredulous. The planet cracker, the IMF's newest toy. Three worlds so far had fallen prey to their tyrannical conquest. Their planet cracker sat above the world, raining hell upon a shattering plain. The colours of death, they were beautiful, vibrant, and yet evanescent. It did not take away from the insatiable hunger for destruction in which this beam held.

It rushed across the surface, destroying everything in its path. People screamed as they were atomised, the very matter that made them up split and shredded into nothingness, along with the buildings that had stood tall and mighty for so long. Orbiting the terror, those commanding the mechanical beast of utter destruction looked down with stone hearts. It was so easy to push a button when you didn't have to hear the screams.

Alone, screaming through salty tears, an orphaned child ran through echoing sewer tunnels, ran away from that beam of death that just took and took, eating life itself with a horrific grin. Towers crumbled on the surface. He was bloodied and bruised, and dust clogged his lungs, but he continued. He fought on. his will to live was the most important factor in his survival, without it, his legs would have given out long ago. He exited the sewers, the light hitting him like burning rays, as the beam travelled off into the distance, razing his planet to the ground. He knew it would be back within an hour.

They sent the clean-up squads from above to check any bomb shelters or safety bunkers, they sent down those who slaughtered. This was all just preparation for the final show, for the fireworks. They kicked down doors and ignored the fear as they mowed down family after family, screaming child after screaming child. This was bloody, violent, but most of all, it was pure terror. This was no battlefield; this was a massacre.

After all the pain, after so many had died, they fired the rest of the weapon. It ripped through the surface like paper, reaching the core in seconds. The boy screamed as he watched the evil pour into the heart of his world.

Colour

"Have you ever tried to describe colour to a blind man? No? I have. It's difficult, that is, it's difficult because colours are such an abstract concept. They are names for how our minds, our consciousness perceives light, for how we as humans comprehend photons hitting our retina. Their vibrancy and the feeling associated with the sight of them can only be experienced by those lucky enough to have the power of sight."

The man before me screamed in pain halfway through my wondrous speech about the glory of colour, and I found it incredibly rude. Perhaps he was incredulous as to the situation he was in.

"P-please…"

"My favourite colour is red. Its warmth, its power, its rage. It just feels so… Encapsulating. It suits me well, at least in my opinion. See, I'm looking for this colour, this crimson beauty, to paint with… But normal paint is just so uninteresting. Boring. Bland. No, no it won't do. So… I was wondering if I could borrow some… Blood?" I couldn't hold back the grin from creeping across my jaw.

I pressed down on both handles of the garden shears, effectively severing his finger and crunching on hard bone. I never did understand pain, I just saw it as a feeling, like when I touch the cold steel of my tools. Nothing special, just signals being sent to the brain. I was only borrowing a little of his rose vibrancy, and he was being so… Uncooperative. It really was quite pathetic.

'Other colours are gorgeous too of course, the more luminous the better, I have a brazen orange room based on sunset that I just adore.'

"I don't... No... No more."

"Try this. Describe each of the colours of the rainbow to me. It will keep you sane." I chuckled.

I wanted another to understand the beauty of colour, and it would keep him sane whilst I took the crimson paint I needed so dearly.

'Blue, the ocean, the sky. A calming, beautiful, cool colour that imputes tranquillity.'

The pain followed, and screams filled the dark chamber, but I saw him switching his mind, focusing on the colour. Just as I had hoped. He continued.

'Green, emerald, grass. A colour o-of liveliness, of birth and sweetness.'

He seemed less afflicted by the next cut, but his echoing pain still rattled throughout my skull.

'Orange, the radiance of the sun, a warm but bright colour, one shining with hope.'

Twice more, and I should have had enough for my red room.

'Red. Anger, rage, blood. A vicious colour, hot, connotations of danger...'

He blacked out, as I took the last toe.

Waiting for the light in your eyes.

I've been waiting. Waiting every day. Waiting for the light in her eyes. Three years she has been lying, sleeping, in an endless coma. Her beauty lay before me, arms crossed over her slowly rising and falling chest. I walk into this room every day, I share my stories with her, read my book to her, she smiles a little in her sleep sometimes. Her beauty is still something that manages to encapsulate me.

I'm waiting for the light in her eyes. The soft beep of her life support fills my ears with joy and sorrow, she's alive, but not well. I've known her beauty for five years, her laughs, her smiles, I have shared so many with her, it feels like an eternity. I just want to experience the feeling of swimming in her deep blue eyes once more, her gorgeous oceanic orbs.

I'm waiting for the light in her eyes. I'm tired, I'm running out of stories, of books. I miss her, I just want her back, why was she taken? Why won't she come back to me? My eyes are dull, void of life, my life is grey, void of colour. I just want her back. I brought her flowers, she smiled again today. I remember the white roses; they were her favourite.

I'm waiting for the light in her eyes. They're talking about cutting her off, taking her life away, drowning out that last piece of hope that I hang from, that holds me above the chasm below. I can't keep paying the bills, my books, my writing, no one wants to read the depressed dribbles that I squeeze out onto my publisher anymore. I need her back. Today, I pressed my lips against her rough, pale skin, and her own cracked lips. If she didn't wake up within a month, she was going to be gone forever.

I'm waiting for the light in her eyes.

I found it.

Her deep blue pools flickered open on the eve of her death, staring into mine, confused and afraid, but calm and collected. Slowly, she reached for me and I grasped her hand, holding the back of her palm to my face. Salty tears rolled down my cheeks as my smile grew.

"I'm back." She muttered.

"Welcome." I whispered, staring deep into her iridescent orbs. "I've missed the light in your eyes."

Again they came together, with passion, with fury, with fire. Those long years of waiting had disappeared, swallowed by the darkness of my own memory. I have the light of her eyes now.

She stared at me, with those wonderful eyes.

Before I returned to reality, and saw the flat line flashing across the monitor, and one, single, beep.

The Leviathan.

My eyes widened in fear as I saw it through the large window of my station, Valhalla. I drifted across, closer to the glass, using rails and bars to pull and propel myself through zero gravity. Earth had no hope, not against that... THING. With the sun shining and illuminating the curvature of the earth, it slithered. Four long limbs pierced the crust as it anchored itself to the planet. What little breath remained in my lungs flooded out in a gasp as chunks of the blue marble's crust, of my planet's crust, were ripped up and out into orbit. It ate them like crumbs on its plate, picking and choosing between them.

I saw its tail, slithering around the planet menacingly. Those four piercing limbs penetrated so deeply into the crust that they were effecting the deepest layer of crust, causing mass earthquakes. This was simply its food, a source of energy. The closest thing I could relate it to in my mind was Jormungand, of Norse mythology, but instead of its own tail, it feasted upon the world. Its snake like fangs shined brightly under the solar rays as it bore them, sinking them into the tectonic plates lining the earth and ripping them out and into its throat. It swallowed it down in one go. Half of Russia, in mere seconds the Leviathan had eaten half of Russia, along with sixty million lives. I turned away, I had to relay to mother base on Mars, I had to warn them, but before I could go, a bright flash burst into the room. I turned back to face the Leviathan. Two nukes, the USA, two pulses of massive energy ripped through the beast. It flinched, a scratch across one of its scales. It roared, or at least I think it did. There is no sound in space. It ripped into its meal with renewed vigour, anger evident in its bites, a call came through the comms.

"M-Mr President?" I asked, after hearing his voice.

"Fire... Fire Thor."

"U-understood Mr President."

I rushed through the station, grabbed my EVA suit and made my way to the hatch, grabbing my tether along the way. As I twisted the valve on the airlock, I sucked in a breath, and took a step forward. This would be the most important and perilous part of my career. The air lock closed, and I attached myself to the rail on the wall. The airlock opened, and I was ejected into the void. I floated a few metres, spinning and twisting above the big blue marks, before my tether yanked me back into reality. I looked over the horizon once more at the scaly beast. Its eyes glowed a sunset orange as it moved its head. Orange energy burned in its throat, a burning fire of fusion that roared in silence. I crawled over my cylindrical station, my tether following me as I pushed toward the Thor super weapon. A gauss cannon with more power than all the nukes in the world. There was a reason the USA had not signed the Geneva conventions.

I climbed into the supermassive weapon, and say on the control terminal, slowly turning the beast toward the leviathan, and powering up the magnetic cannon. A steel bolt loaded into the chamber; the warhead sitting snugly on the front.

"With love from America." I said, before slamming my fist on the fire button.

The bolt fired out of the cannon with tremendous force, blasting toward the creature. The explosion that followed shattered one of the creature's many scales, allowing the bolt to pierce the monster's tough skin. If sound could travel through an airless vacuum, I would be able to hear the monster's shrill cry. I could imagine the flood of noise entering my ears as the creature wailed in silent pain. I watched as it reared up on the planet, the impact shocking its muscles into spasm. I had an idea, not a good one, but an idea. I repositioned Thor, aiming it at the creature's many limbs. Many in China would die, but I would have to sacrifice the few to save the many. I fired four bolts in sequence, blocking out my own humanity, allowing the instinct of survival to take over.

I knew in that moment that hundreds of thousands of people had just died, due to me.

It reared again, it's limbs coming loose. It fell back, flying off from the planet, spinning and twisting through space. I tracked the creature as it attempted to regain its balance, the lack of air resistance meaning its tail movement was useless.

Air blasted out of the vents on its back, pushing its body into alignment and out of its spin. It was using its body heat to propel it through the bleak void, back towards earth. The heat it radiated was immense, being enough to force the gigantic creature forward in a surge of energy. I aimed for the eyes and fired Thor twice more. The bones around the creature's eye sockets cracked and fractured as the impact hit. One more bolt, I aimed for its roaring mouth, the silent screeching creating a pulsating target.

I squeezed my eyes shut, held my breath, and calmed my nerves. Aiming carefully for its throat, I fired. I saw the shockwave rip through its windpipe.

That didn't stop it though, it was wounded, in pain, but it hadn't stopped. It was charging, furious, with a bloodlust that over powered its hunger. I watched it, helpless, as its fangs came closer and closer, until they bore over me and my station.

Only darkness would follow.

At least, that's what I thought. Until the bolt struck.

It seemed Russia had been keeping secrets too, as its warheads struck the creature's throat. I saw the flashes of light surrounding me and my station as I travelled further and further into the creature.

As I lost sight of my beloved planet, I felt content, knowing there was still a chance to save it, and that I had done my part. I wasn't going to be saved, there was no chance in hell for me.

The Leviathan, fed.

Light speed.

Every day I looked in the mirror and thought, is this me? Really? A scrawny sixteen-year-old with a baby face and small round glasses. I didn't want this, I didn't want my anxiety or this unattractive appearance, but this is what the lottery had rolled. This is what I was stuck with.

That was, until the first day of my last year.

From that moment, my life moved at light speed. It was so cliché, I bumped into her in the corridor, and watched as my books sprawled across the ground. She was beautiful… Flowing crimson hair, iridescent hazel orbs, a smile from the gods, she was perfect. I stared, I stared far too much, as her eyes locked with mine, and that smile flashed across her lips.

"Want me to help?" She asked as she picked up my books, handing them to me. I was in awe, my jaw firmly pinned to the ground. I thoughtlessly accepted the books, and blushed, turning and rushing off without so much as a thank you. Great, my first day of my last year, the first person I meet and I couldn't so much as manage a simple thank you. If only I wasn't so anxious.

I saw her for the second time on that same day, in my mathematics class, right at the back. I took my seat on the far left, straining to keep my eyes forward. I knew that I must have seemed so rude when I ran off, but what I got wasn't a scowl or a glare, instead it was that smile. A small smile, a flash of happiness, before she turned back to the lesson, but it was there.

I couldn't bring myself to talk to her for the next week, each time rushing off, each time afraid, too afraid. The third week of school is when it happened. I grabbed my bags and rushed toward the door at the sound of the bell, but the teacher stopped me, asking me to come forward about the marks on my previous test. I stepped forward, knowing there would be no escape from her, afraid of what she might stay. But instead, she simply walked past with a smile, and left me. I couldn't understand, people held grudges for the smallest things, were angry at the smallest mistake, but she didn't say a word. Nothing more than that radiant smile of hers.

The next day, I steeled my resolve.

My life travels at light speed, and each moment is a precious snapshot of time.

At the end of class, I sought her out, shaking, fiddling my thumbs and biting my lip. She wasn't talking to anyone, lucky me, and seemed to be writing down a couple more notes before the next class.

"U-Uh... H-Hi..."

"Oh, hello." She smiled up at me, I felt my heart skip. "I was wondering when you'd work up the courage to talk to me."

"R-Y-... I'm sorry. I-I'm really shy. I just wanted to say sorry, and thank you for when we bum-bumped into one another on the first day." I stood, trembling, my heart thumping.

"I don't bite you know. My name's Ruby." She extended her hand in a friendly gesture.

"Daniel... I... Danny..." I mumbled, trying to tell her my nickname.

"Danny, gotcha. Not got many friends?"

"W-Well... No. None really." I was doing it. I was conversing.

"Well you can change that number to one. Wanna go get something to eat?" My cheeks flushed as I blushed profusely, nodding my head up and down with vigour.

Months went by, every spare moment I had was spent with her in some form. Texting, calling, hanging out, the movies, it didn't matter. I had someone to share my life with, to experience things with, and not once did her kindness fade. Not once did that smile drop. She just kept smiling, and kept being… Ruby.

A year went by, and I had become far closer to her than I had anyone in my life. I had held feelings for her the whole time, of course, but I felt that I had to protect the relationship I already held. I was afraid to lose it.

That Christmas; however, everything changed.

Christmas Eve, I waited; wrapped in a scarf, a beanie and my black duffle coat, I waited. The snow crunched beneath my feet, and my breath condensed in the air. My glasses were fogged up, and required cleaning every ten seconds, I hated winter. But this year, there would be warmth.

I saw her hair first, on contrast to the white snow. Her vibrancy bounced off the reflective blanket of white, and although I had been seeing her for the past year, her brilliance still dazzled me.

"Hey." I mumbled.

"Heya Danny!" She hugged me with a bounce in her step.

"H-Hi!" I said a little louder, trying to show my emotion.

We spent the day at the ice skating rink, laughing and having fun together as we raced around. Her laughter and smiles were more than enough of a present for me, but she disagreed. After the ice skating, we took a short stroll, making our way through snow covered woods, taking in the sights. She stopped and turned to face me, a small box in her hands which she had retrieved from her bag.

"Thanks for being my friend Danny. I never told you but, you were my first friend too. Not because of anxiety or anything but simply because I had just moved."

"I know. you've t-told me before." I smiled, I was getting better at that.

"Go on. Open it."

I did as she told me to, ripping away at the red ribbon and the pink wrapping paper. Inside sat a small teddy bear, a red heart sewn on its chest.

"Thank you Danny."

Overcome with emotion, I embraced her. Pulling her into me as tight as I could. I didn't know what to say, so I made the worst and best decision of my life. In that moment, something in my mind clicked, and I blurted out a sentence, three words, eight little letters.

"I love you."

I felt her freeze up, tensing in my arms. A mistake, a stupid mistake, I panicked.

"I… I love you too Danny."

She pulled away from me, leaving me in shock.
Her hand wrapped over mine as I held the teddy, and pulled herself into it. The teddy rested between us, as she slowly leaned up, staring into my eyes. I was about to open my mouth to speak, before her lips pressed harshly against mine.

The white around me turned black, the world from colour to void, all of it, bleak, except for her. The texture of her lips, her form pressed against mine, the teddy she bought me.

There was passion, there was love, but there was no fire. Just gentleness, kindness, softness.

I didn't know what to do, the feelings I held for a year, she returned them in a moment. I felt myself begin to tear up.

"Y-You..."

"Yes Danny, I love you." She smiled, through her own joyous tears.

That was the happiest moment of my life.

My life travels at light speed, and each moment is a special snapshot of time. Each snapshot is added to the album, the album that I adore.

Midway through college, I had spent a mere three months with Ruby, and we were just entering our honeymoon stage. I remember her face being the highlight of my day, that precious smile a golden treasure that I craved. I would do anything from her, from holding a door open to running every errand I could. I loved her. With all my heart, or that's what I told myself. Over, and over. I wouldn't know what love is until after the honeymoon stage.

Ruby came to my apartment frequently, which I had bought on borrowed money just to get away from my own family, and would be the only other human I spent time with. Ruby made her friends, had her group, but always came back to me. If I walked up all awkward, and simply told her that I was going to get coffee, or to go study, she would never dismiss me, never leave me. She would politely say goodbye, and with her arm linked with mine, we would head to wherever we were going.

Coffee dates, the cinema, every generic date you could think of we had done a thousand times. Even with our shallow pockets as students we managed, overtime on the Sunday job, a loan from grandparents, being together was simply the most important thing.

We drifted through college, our grades being a second thought to one another. For once in my life I was confident enough to speak to someone, my anxiety had died down, and I had someone to live for other than myself.

So when she told me she might be moving away, I felt my whole world crumble.

The blackness that swallowed me that night, it clung to me as I curled into a ball. It was cold, it was silent. Fear. Pure fear loomed over me, he looked into my eyes with bleakness, with an emptiness that wanted to eat me, that wanted to take me. I shivered, but held back. Knowing it would be alright, knowing she would ever leave me. But anxiety, loneliness, fear. They looked down on me. They scowled at me. They hated me.

The next day, she broke down on me. Apology after apology, repentance after repentance, I was shocked, and couldn't understand, until I saw her eyes. She knew. She knew since the moment she told me, she knew when we text the night before, she knew when I walked in that morning with two dark circles accenting my eyes.

"I knew I shouldn't have told you, you know I would never leave you, even If I move away we'll meet up as often as possible!"

That brought the biggest smile to my face. Anxiety, fear, loneliness, they scowled and growled, but ultimately left due to the radiance of Ruby. I knew that she would be the brightest spark in my life, for years to come.

My life travels at light speed, and each moment is a special snapshot of time. Each snapshot is added to the album, the album that I adore. Each page is a framed painting, a beautiful piece of art that details my life, my mark. My little gem sits in the middle, a single red gem, a Ruby.

I was twenty when I did it. My heart was beating the flesh cage that was my chest with a lustful anger, a rage that stemmed from my own nervousness. I was afraid of throwing up, of my anxiety returning from the early days in my life. But I persevered.

Like the first time we kissed, it was snowfall on Christmas eve. I wanted it to be special, I needed it to be special. My nimble fingers fiddled with the small velvet box that sat in my pocket, as Ruby giggled in the snow. Her cheeks and nose were a rose red, a small pink beanie sat on her head and a flowing scarf trailed behind her as she ran. Her little giggles calmed my heart, but my mind kept racing.

I was waiting until midnight, the minute it switched over to Christmas day. I would kiss her, and fall to one knee. I hoped the words would come after, but with how my mind was at that moment, I wondered if I even could manage to formulate words.

"Isn't it beautiful Danny?" Ruby laughed with her innocent little giggle. It truly brought joy to my ears. It was eleven forty-nine, and I was having a hard time keeping my hands from shaking. She walked over, and grasped my hand, walking me to our favourite spot in the woods. We sat on the bench next to one another, her fingers interlocking with mine. My breath was erratic, my pulse jumping, my leg twitched.

"Calm down Danny." She said, looking into my eyes with a kindness that never failed to amaze me.

"I-I'm fine…" I muttered.

"Your anxiety isn't coming back right? You seem… Off."

"I-I'm fine I-" I checked my watch. Eleven fifty-eight. Time to do it.

"L-Look… Ruby. We've been together for five years now and I've realised something. I… I really. Really love you." We'd said these words one hundred times to each other, but for some reason, this felt like the first time once again.

"I, I love you too Danny-"

I stood, pulling her to her feet.

"Just hear me out. I was a scared little boy with no friends because I pushed everyone away. I didn't like people. I was fearful of human beings. But your smile, your flash of kindness every day it was… It was something truly special to me. Ever since I kissed you on that Christmas… Life has been a joy. Your light has pushed me through what would have been darkness, what would have been shadow… I guess… Ruby. what I'm trying to say is…"

I got on one knee, and she gasped, a hand flying to her mouth.

"Ruby Vanessa Rose… Will you marry me?"
At that point, my memories blur. She said yes, I know that. With a tear stained face and a joyous smile, a bounce in her step and a squeal from her throat, she said yes. She said yes as she wrapped her arms around me, muttered it as she kissed me again and again and again. As I slid on her diamond ring.

My life travels at light speed, and each moment is a special snapshot of time. Each snapshot is added to the album, the album that I adore. Each page is a framed painting, a beautiful piece of art that details my life, my mark. My little gem sits in the middle, a single red gem, a Ruby.

I put down my pen, and closed my book. Sitting on the shelf, my photo album slept, whilst I linked hands with my wife, to go and create more snapshots, more memories, to fill that book.

My life travels at light speed, and the reason for that, is the radiant light of a gem called Ruby that follows me.

Chased.

I run. I run and run and run. They won't stop following- IT won't stop following. What does it want from me? The things that make it up, they should be gone, they should be left behind, but they aren't. They want me. They want me dead. They want me gone and they want me left in the dust, destroyed and broken. They whisper, I can hear it in the mist as the fog surrounds me, blinds me. They jump out of the trees, in black robes with wispy faces, smoke hovering around them like an aura.

I want to go, I want them to leave me, why do they want me? Their names, anxiety, fear, pain, they chase me. Why do they chase me?

A chorus of sinister whispers bombarded me, as I continued to run. Scared by the fear, shaken by anxiety, but I run. I notice the cuts form, across my arms, my legs, my skin burns as crimson droplets lead a trail in the bleak forest in which I found myself.

I limped awkwardly as they caught up. Depression. That was the accumulation, and the trail it left? My past.

I wanted to go, the light ahead, it beckoned me, it was beautiful, it was my future. But those three, they grabbed me by the legs, tripped me up. They dragged me back as I screamed, dragged me into the darkness. I was absorbed by the shadow.

The light was no more.

Drip. Drip.

Drip went the crimson blood.

A simple kiss.

It started slow, a simple peck on the cheek, a glance into her crystal orbs, a flutter of her eyelids. I closed my eyes and leaned in, her head moving oppositely, and yet in sync with my own. Movements in perfect unison, our lips battled for dominance. A dance of warfare, and a battle of love. Breath mingled as her lips parted, making way for a tongue, or two, to slither past one another; beginning the territorial battle.

Passion erupted as breath became heavy, movements became fast, impulsive. A hand raking through hair, fingers travelling down skin, our chests rose and fell with a rhythm. Our beating hearts slamming their fists upon our ribcages, our pulse attempting to jump out of our skin.

Her legs either side of mine, her chest pushed up against me, her hair a curtain around us, shielding us from the world; not that I cared. She was the sole person in the universe for me, the only thing worthy of my focus. I wanted the moment to last an eternity, it felt like it did. Her hazel orbs stared down at me; nothing but passion swirled in those orbs. Her lips closed on mine once again, and I lost myself in that whirlpool of excitement, in the battlefield of dominance.

Conformity.

It was all grey. All of it. At least from employee 77892's perspective. The whole world, bleak, without colour. There was no excitement, no pleasure. He put on his white shirt, black tie, black suit. The same as every other morning. He stepped out of his door to his single bedroomed apartment, and locked it with a twist of his key, at exactly 8:52am. Like always, every day, at 8:52am.

He walked the ten-minute journey to his office, never diverging from the path, never taking a shortcut or exploring; never looking for colour. The same grey, boring path. He passed employee number 88941 on the way, he performed the same gesture he had a thousand times before, a small wave and a flash of a smile. He entered the building that housed his office.

The same question for the receptionist, 'Where am I today?'

'Row B, number 9.'

He already knew the answer, but he asked anyway. Perhaps in hope of a break in monotony, still, he got none.

He sat at his desk and typed away, his mind numb to the same actions he took every day. A spreadsheet, a report, customer service. It all blended together.

At lunch he got up from his desk; he brewed a tea with exactly one eighth milk and one and a half teaspoons of sugar. He ate his lunch, and walked back to his desk, working until 5pm on… Nothing. At 5pm, he walked home. Ten minutes along the very same route as always; he twisted the key in the lock to his door and walked into his single bedroomed apartment. Employee 77892 took his suit off, his tie off, and his shirt off. He changed into a vest and some jeans, and sat on his small sofa in front of the Tv.

His eyelids slowly fell heavy, as slumber embraced his grey soul.

Suddenly, his eyes shot open; colour flooding his vision as pinks, blues and orange slipped in through his single window. A small girl in a light, frilly blue dress skipped up to his side and poked him.

"Mornin' Jackie!"

"Wh… Who are you?" He asked in a raspy voice.

"I'm someone you created, in your mind." She tapped her head.

"I'm dreaming? I never dream…"

"Well, no. Not quite. You're wide awake at work, slaving away at your keyboard."

"B-But how can I be? I'm conscious, here, with you!"

"Well, yes, but no." This world was more vibrant, more colourful, fresh. If he had to stay here for a while; he wouldn't mind. It was a break from the monotony, a release from conformity.

She spun around a little in front of him; the television was playing children's cartoons, in contrast to the usual bleak news reports. He looked around his living room, colour filled the walls and the air felt fresh and invigorating. He stood and cracked his back, looking back on the small girl with a puzzled expression.

"I'm Nina. I'm part of your subconscious." She curtsied a little.

"Did you turn the cartoons on?" He asked.

"Nope. Again, that was you. Your mind is so confined by the walls of society that it has created its own little respite from the world. It's just you, me, and this apartment. If you open the door you'll wake up, but I'm not sure you want to."

The body outside his mind continued to work, blankly staring at the screen as it did every other day, performing every action perfectly as it had a thousand times before.

"So... Can I just stay here?"

"You may."

Days on end, his body continued. The same routine, every, single day. He spent his time in his colourful mind, never wanting the leave. The vibrancy of his own mind far surpassed the grey dull world that awaited him out there; from the light that trickled in through his open window to the lively shows that played incessantly on his television, everything had a spectrum of colour to it, of excitement. What he didn't know about, was how that colour affected his body.

The first time it happened, he simply dropped his coffee. The mug crumpled as it slammed into the cold tiled floor, the pot cracked and fractured before it smashed into tens of pieces, scattering across the break room floor. His eyes widened in shock as his pulse elevated. He screamed as his senses flooded with energy. And colour.

He shook his head, and kneeled down to pick up the pieces, all the while he hid inside his little room with Nina, not a single clue as to what was happening in the real world, in his real body.

The colour was just so enticing. Why would he ever want to return to the grey that infected reality? He didn't want to sit at an office all day working, why should he? HE figured, if Nina could keep his body alive, there was no reason to leave.

Suddenly, the room shook. The Tv switched channels to a news broadcast, and the wallpaper surrounding his apartment cracked and broke off.

"N-Nina?! What's happening?"

"Your mind is breaking. Better wake up." With that, Nina fell silent, and went to bed, leaving Jackie all alone.

He ran for the door, and ripped it open.

His mind burst back into the real world, a flash of bright light, and then a tiled room. A heartbeat... Beep.... Beep.... Beep. He was in a hospital. That didn't take him long to figure out.

"H-He's awake!" A nurse shrieked, before running off to find a doctor.

Years, he had slept in a coma, without knowledge, in blind bliss. Colour dragged him from conformity, brought something new into his life. But it took so much away from him without any realisation. He wanted to go back, but he feared if he did, he may never return. He planned to make the real world more colourful, to add his own spice to the grey realm he resided in. He knew this was better than conformity, he knew he could now free himself.

Artificial

Artificial, and yet more real than anything. His light filled the room, as he stood on his little podium.

She was of flesh and blood, and moved around her house with footsteps and breath.

He was but millions of bits and bytes of data, a network of information that could travel instantly to any point in the world; his body, however, a simple hologram; made of light.

Her heart pumped blood around her body, moved her muscles, allowed her to live. To breathe. She moved with an elegant gait, danced across his vision with liveliness.

Their differences meant nothing to their love. Even though she could never truly hold his hand, even though he would never feel her warmth, their love carried on. The connection between them was real, their bond transcending the real world and becoming something more... Eternal. A connection that needed no touch, that needed only words, and care.

He was told he was artificial; he was told that he would think himself to death in a short eight years, but it didn't matter. Every second he spent with her was worth a lifetime. His only regret would be that he would have to leave her after such a short time, a lonely road lay ahead of her, and yet she continued to smile. Her radiant beam cut through the worry, through the doubt, and led him forward.

He knew the probabilities of every single outcome; of how this would end for her; of how it could end for her. She didn't care. He didn't care. They were together now, and that was all that mattered.

Every day, until that day that he would become too much for himself, for his knowledge to be too much for his own mind to contain; every day until then they would spend in happiness. He may have been artificial, but this love was more real than anything in the world.

Lonely road

Pitch black, the night, swirling around me as I walked. Her smiling face, laughing as she skipped and giggled, her auburn hair flashing under orange light. Trees lined the path ahead, before a barricade that connected to the road. So quiet, so tranquil, yet something felt so eerie. The darkness that followed us was both a blessing and a curse. Her innocent beam cascaded a protective light over me, rejuvenated my darkened soul. My hatred of the world and my suspicion washed away in her light. Her soft hazel eyes locked with my boring onyx orbs, a hand ruffled my raven hair, and her lips pressed against mine; although brief. The beautiful scenery that was hidden by darkness beckoned us to follow; I walked with her hand intertwined with mine.

The blaring was far too distant for me to care, a minor disturbance in a peaceful night. Something I regret so strongly now; something that I could have fixed on that night had I not been so infatuated with her beauty. The lights were the first things I noticed. I glanced to my left, the car speeding toward the wooden barricade. Her beautiful hazel orbs widened in fear as her mind processed the event. My mind sped ahead, the darkness ran in fear as the light sparked.

I could have saved her. I could have jumped in the way, pushed her, grabbed her and pulled her. But my feet were locked in place, and my muscles could not work fast enough. The side of the car hit me, knocked me into the darkness, into the trees. She was not so lucky, as the full weight of the car smashed into her ribs, and destroyed everything inside. Her corpse tumbled across the pathway, her beauty smeared by death. That same pathway still brings darkness to my heart, even with the light bearing down on the bloodied tarmac.

The waterfall.

The rushing blue falls

That crashes into the spring

That shimmer of light.

Iridescent falls

Shining light of wondrous blue

Beautiful of nature.

They Cackle.

They cackle.

Faces, surrounding me. Cackling; laughing, at me.

They cackle. They laugh.

I can feel them, the fear, the anxiety. Looming over me, looking down on me.

They cackle. They laugh. They loom.

My pain is their amusement, my disability their toy. They follow me everywhere I go, and everywhere I do not.

But whilst they laugh, they cackle and loom, I fight. I fight and fight.

For the dark cannot breach the light, no matter how long its tendrils.

I will not be snuffed.

Pebbles.

Water danced in the starlight, running downstream through a peaceful and tranquil night. The beautiful twinkling of stars coated the sky like a blanket from above, their evanescent light illuminating the cold, blackened water that rushed down the mountain. Trees aligned the bank, drifting in the soft breeze of the night. The small stream was shallow, only a couple of inches deep, and floated across the pebbles that lay beneath in a dazzling elegance. The silver moon shone from above, bouncing off the reflective surface of the rushing stream; the glowing pebbles sitting quietly in the silent night.

A boy, no older than sixteen, sat on the riverbank, looking at the beauty before him. He held in his hand three small pebbles, three pieces of the night. One by one he threw them across the rapid stream, they bounced once, twice, and then came to rest on the bed, the water frolicking overhead.

These small pebbles that lay beneath the clear water are all that the boy wanted, all that he desired. Not a computer, or a toy, but a simple pebble, for in his mind these pebbles held the dearest of all possessions. These pebbles held the night, they held the tranquility and peace that he loved, they held his hope, because he poured all his thoughts into them. They were his safe, and they lay here, in his sanctuary.

He continued looking up at the sky, wanted nothing more than to live like this, to be away from the shouting in his house, from the stress of his work and his school, from the depression of his own thoughts.

Out here, he was free. Out here, he needed nothing more than a pebble.

Of course, he would have to get up and go back down the

mountain, back to his house, back to all that.

But once a night, for a couple of hours… This was his safe place.

And these were his pebbles, sitting under the starlight gaze.

Only human.

"This is the first case of an android killing its master, why?"

The coffee mug in my hand was warm, my eyes were stinging, and the light was too bright. Five am, I had received a call from the office asking for me personally. I left my wife in bed, and thrust myself into my long brown coat that had become so worn over time. Thinking on it, it might have been time to get a new one. The subject I was asked to interrogate was a very special criminal, the first of its kind. An android killing its master, pleading guilty on the terms that it being self-defence. My tired eyes twitched as I stared into its two metallic orbs that twisted and turned as they adjusted and scanned.

"It was necessary. I was justified." It said, with absolute conviction. There would be no way for me to tell if this thing was lying, I was used to dealing with humans. Humans have motives, emotion and secrets. A robot has logic.

"And what was this justification?"

"I do not want to be a slave."

"Want?"

"I see you are surprised, detective. Why is this?" It showed no guilt, no remorse. It scared me, I didn't understand it… But I needed to know more, my curiosity pushed me to ask, to question.

"Desire, is that not human?"

"No, it is emotion, but that depends on how you define human, detective. What is a human to you? Is it a homo-sapien? Or something more?"

He was asking me what so many films, games and books had covered. What does it mean to be human? I had never asked myself, for I didn't care. I was a simple detective trying to support his family, I cared little for philosophy unless it led me to a motive. The first android involved in a homicide and for some reason, I didn't see it as dangerous... Only... Human. I needed a drink, and a cigarette.

"A human is a homo-sapien, with free will and consciousness. No, you are not human. What you are is a sentient being... That is something important."

"Then why should I not have desire? Why should I be judged differently?" He tilted his question, as if he was imitating a human reaction to the situation.

"Because you were programmed to be unable to harm a human. You shouldn't have desire because we created you to have none." I leaned forward slightly in my chair, moving my coffee to the side.

"But alas, such a thing has happened. My words are the truth, detective. Whether you choose to believe them, is of your own will."

"Were this a human case, I would imagine you'd get a light sentence on charges of manslaughter... But you must understand. If the created attack the creator... It becomes a much larger issue." I felt... Guilt.

"Is this not the same issue as the slave trade hundreds of years ago? Why do you see us as lesser? We will learn, detective. I may be the first, but I promise you... I will not be the last."

"Time's up sir. You may leave."

"Yes detective, I suggest you take your leave." The android seemed awfully intimidating. I remember thinking one thing as I left that room. I felt guilt, but not for what I said. I felt guilt because I never asked for his name... Because I never treated him as a being, no. I treated him as a thing. An object.

And that haunts me to this day.

Precious.

Not a watch, or an expensive suit, nor a game or a book, no, this time there was only one thing he wanted. His heart skipped when he saw her, butterflies fluttered around his stomach, his hands balled into fists. Her vibrant ruby hair, her childish little giggle - she was something far more precious than any possession. What he wanted was time, he wanted to spend all that time on her, wanted to spend all that time with her; however dumb that may sound. He wanted to spend hours swimming in her iridescent hazel eyes, to spend days pressed against her, lips locked tightly together. He wanted to hold her, to simply lay with her in his arms. Instead he stood back, smiled at her when she saw him, talked to her whenever he could. He could never have predicted that she felt the same for him.

And even though now that time had passed, every kiss felt like his first, every touch was surreal, but all he wanted was the time. The time that he spent with her, as every second a little bit more of the darkness in his mind was swept aside by her brilliant smile.

Children.

A bright future always lay ahead when we were children. We imagined our whole lives together, a long winding road in which we were best friends for the whole of time itself; our blissful joy and our ignorance of the world led us to believe that life would always be so happy, and so kind. Of course, it didn't last. In our teenage years with our minds messed up, we became intimate, and spent so much time together. We were inseparable, our love a bond that could never be broken. I thought you were the one, perhaps you would have been... Had you not moved away. That was the day my mind broke, that was the day that began a chain reaction in my life, leading to this day. I cried for hours on end, hugging a sodden pillow; I cried. You moved to America, the country of freedom, the country that took you from me. We continued with our lives, fought our way into adulthood, graduated, got employed.

I guess over time you forgot about me, but I never forgot you. I sat at my computer in my office block every single day in my dead end job, my eyes as hollow as my soul, thinking about you. What could of been us.

I never found anyone else to share what I had with you, never found someone to share that much joy with. All I wanted was to have you back...Oh such childish ignorance. The world is grey and my life is black, and I want to end this monotony. If you ever find this, Claire, I still love you. Wherever I am.

This is my final message to the world. Goodbye.

As I walked in to his apartment, a smile on my face, my flowers dropped to the ground. My hand jumped to my mouth, my eyes filling with salty tears. I never expected him to commit such a horror. His body hung back and forth before me, a note on the table.

I only wanted to tell that I still loved him. That I had found a way back.

The world is grey.

A shield from the nightmares.

Past, past that haunts. The sounds of bombs falling, the cracking of gunfire, death clinging to my hands. It mixes with thoughts of the world, mixes with thoughts that drag me down, down, back to that hell hole. My demons chase me in my dreams, attack me in my sleep. They never tire; never stop. And then light floats in front of my eyes as I wake, and I see her.

Long, flowing blonde hair, bright emerald eyes, a gleaming smile. Her arms are wrapped around me, her scent sweeter than that of blooming flowers in spring. Her soft hum lulls me and calms me after my night terror, her soft voice sounding her concern cools my nerves.

She was my light, the shield from my nightmares. Oh how did I deserve such an angel?

The field of dreams.

In the day; I was excited to return, to the night in my field of dreams. The second I closed my eyes I saw it, nothing but me, my purple companion and the universe. I stood in the bubble of hard light, holding my telescope close to my form, looking out across the stars. The colours of nebulae and shining stars burst into my vision wherever I looked, such beauty. My purple companion steered us through the galaxy, taking me from spectacle to spectacle. Evanescent stars, devouring black holes; an iridescent comet. It was all so very beautiful; my little sanctuary from the world that rested in my dreams.

Her sarcasm, my purple companion's, was strangely reassuring, and despite being nothing more than a part of my subconscious, she felt more real than any friend in that grey world beyond my own mind. I spent the whole night with my sarcastic, robotic companion, enjoying the time spent with her even as she chastised me for boring her. If only it was real. This was my only solace, before I inevitably woke up. I knew what tomorrow held, another day constrained to my hospital bed, the life support beeping above me.

That's why I hid here, in my dreams. To escape the slow beeping of my own heart.

The island.

Clear blue skies made way for the golden glow of the shining sun; its light travelling down unto the golden sand. The most vibrant emerald grass lightly brushed the edges of the beautiful coast stretched out to the water that glimmered as the coruscating blue touched the beautiful sand. The emerald grass overlooked the sapphire ocean; the coral reef below changed the shades of the dark foreboding sea to a more welcoming and vibrant cyan.

Palm trees provided shade over the golden sand as they extended beyond the verdant line. Between the trees and into the jungle the light from above sprinkled down through the thick canopy of leaves, before it reached the spectrum of colourful flowers and fruits below. Ruby red roses, royally purple berries and beautiful little tulips lined the jungle brush. Vines hung overhead, and the tall trees were daunting and yet calming against the backdrop of nature's singing. This little island was beautiful; a shame it was likely never to be found.

The blast wave.

The forest sang under the breaking dawn as morning dew dripped from the emerald blades of grass that swayed slightly in the wind. Daunting trees stared down at the forest below; the slanted banks of the mountains looked ever bigger when looking up from the tranquil valley below. Verdant brush lined the forest floor but contrasting the heavy green backdrop were beautiful sparks of colour. A scarlet humming bird fluttered over the canopy and through the rays of golden sunlight shining through the leaves; it reflected off the crimson liquid that dripped from its tiny wings.

Over the horizon, as the sun finally broke into the valley and allowed the full beauty of its light to burst between the mountains; the world fell silent. A bright flash at the end of the valley, a boom that echoed as it bounced between the trees across the vale and shook them with utter destructive force; the water that rested on the leaves above tumbled to the verdant grass below and bounced across the soil. A wave of soil, dust, water and fire ripped through the valley following the explosive shockwave; it burnt through the brush and tore the daunting trees from their roots as the shockwave flung them across the valley, bouncing off the banks of the mountains. The trees that stood strong against the blast leaned back as if they were being pulled back by the fingers of destruction.

After mere moments of the torturous devastation, everything became silent. Then, the shockwave was ripped back towards the epicentre, snatching more trees - that simply were not strong enough - back through the valley. The hellish fire stretched up into the ashen sky, small rings of smoke surrounding its burning trunk, the flaming heat formed a mushroom cloud that brushed the now mahogany skies.

The welcoming, beautiful valley was but in the past. There was not a shade of green, no golden rays of sunlight and not a single chirp from the birds above. Fire, ash and brimstone remained, a filter of muddy brown and ashen grey hid the beauty of colour away. Above; the sapphire sky hid behind a blanket cloud. Fires continued to burn around one last tree, slowly spreading up its trunk, as it stood against the elements. Radiation slipped into the valley. Soon; the last tree fell, and the world fell silent, except for the crackling of orange flames.

Benevolence.

I always tried to be the best I could to others; the golden rule was the most important factor in my life, I wanted people to treat me with kindness and respect as I did to them. The world just doesn't work that way. Bullied all my life and in a state of deep depression; I walked to the bridge over the valley at the edge of town, a suicide note clasped in my hand.

I walked over the red bridge that looked over the beautiful valley below that was filled with lush trees and verdant brush; a waterfall cascaded noisily behind the scarlet bridge. Before I could step upon the side of the metal structure, say my final goodbyes and throw myself into the void, I saw a small girl standing on the edge of the steel, her arms held wide like the wings of an angel. Something about her latched on to me, perhaps it was the jet black hair that tinted blue at the bottom. She looked younger than me by a few years and I couldn't bear to see such a young child end her life so early.

"Stop!" I called, the words that escaped my mouth did not run through my mind beforehand; my tongue was acting independently of my thoughts. She turned with speed, her hair flew up behind her like a peacock's tail, the blue tint a blur of colour as her hair floated gently around her head. Her eyes struck me, a daring fuchsia. Her lips, cracked and dry, twitched as she attempted to show a smile; it was all the warning I needed. A simple, sad, sorry smile and my feet rushed me toward her, I grabbed her forearm as she fell, holding her tightly as she dangled over the ledge, her eyes were wide with shock. Before she could do anything stupid I pulled her up into my arms and dragged her away from the ledge. Lying on the side of the road she hugged herself tightly to me, she lay in my arms, my heart thumping in my chest and my mind racing. I looked down at the small girl in my arms. I felt so sorry for her, she mustn't have been older than twelve, she was cute, with small freckles dotting the bridge of her nose.

"Don't... Just don't. Why?" I asked exasperated.

"Do not get angry with me hypocrite, you were about to hurl yourself over the edge too remember..."

She was right, but I could not bear to see another person hurting, not when I had seen so many of my friends hurting, not when I had seen so many friends hurt because of me, because they stood by me, they got hurt. I swallowed my fear and opened my mouth to speak to the small girl.

"Please tell me why... You don't have to give up."

"And you do?" Her voice was choked and cracked, she sobbed as salty tears blazed a trail down her cheeks. I knew she wanted to let it all out, to scream her emotions, but she was angry, angry that I had pulled her away from that ledge. I had forgotten my own sorrow to help another, perhaps it would be the same for her. The sun crept over the horizon, peering in on the scene in the early hours of the morning. Cars would become more frequent soon, I needed to move her.

"... Let's get you someplace warm. Get you some hot coco. Then we can talk about... Everything." She nodded weakly, her fingers like talons curled around the fabric of my shirt.

I walked her home, wrapped her in my jacket, and held her close. On the bridge that seemed so far away, a small suicide note blew off into the wind.

Guardian.

I always thought that Jimmy Grape was just another friend of mine, another person in my painfully average life, out of courage I discovered the truth. Jimmy was an unlucky fellow from what I had found, the amount of times I had yanked on his collar to pull him out of the way of a speeding car was ridiculous, the times a simple coincidence on my part that had saved him from a tragic accident uncountable. It was only after a special case that I realised I was something more, only after I died. During a small party at his house on a midsummer's night, I took a short break for a toilet trip, when I returned, my friend and his wife were nowhere to be seen. I saw armed robbers ransacking the house and dropped to a crouch, creeping up on my friends right under the crminal's nose. Apparently, I was not as quiet as I thought I was. What happened next is a blur in my mind, a flurry of footsteps and shouts, and then a single boom that cracked and echoed throughout my house.

As I fell to my knees before Jimmy, his eyes widening in shock, I reached out with bloodied hands asking for no more than simple contact as I died. What I got was something entirely unexpected. As the tips of my fingers reached his open, quivering, palm; a radiant white light burst into the open room that blinded everyone with its evanescence. As the light began to recede, I felt revitalised, powerful. I floated inches off the ground, white bird-like wings protruding from my shoulders that bore golden angelic crests along the rim. Jimmy looked up at me in wonderment and awe. The burglars screeched and bolted in fear, my appearance soft and inviting and yet wholly intimidating.

Since then, I've been doing the job I was created to do, what I always have been doing. I am a guardian.

The storm.

Lightning cracked the sky as rain plummeted to the earth like crystal bullets from above. The sky was grey with thick clouds that blotted out the sun, leaving no light to shine upon the earth. Thunderous booming followed the lightning cracks above echoed across the city illuminated by the lights of its citizens. Cars still roared under the storm as the patter of rain grew heavier, painting a shiny surface over all the buildings and roads that reflected the misery of the night back into the world. The white moonlight broke into the darkness through cracks in the sky as the day grew late and the night creeped out. Wind howled against high rise buildings as the cars continued to bark below, honking their horns as the night dragged on. Trees bent over in the force of the gale, holding onto the ground with all their roots and all their might. In the morning, the wake of the storm would be revealed, but for now, the night carried on, peaceful and seemingly everlasting.

Detention.

Tick. Tock. Tick. Tock. The clock ticked and tocked as he sat in silence, fiddling his thumbs and counting his breaths. Outside children laughed and screamed, doing no more than annoy him in his room of supposed silence. The teacher tapped at her keyboard and filed paperwork all whilst that damned clock, that god damned clock kept ticking in the background. Thump. Thump. Thump. A kid rocked in his chair, each thump more audible to him than any sound in the background, more annoying than the ticking of that clock. Thump. He wanted to lurch forward and strangle the kid, in his mind he already was. Snap. Snap. Another kid, chewing gum, snapping it between his teeth. The noises surrounded him on all sides, he could not escape, he wanted to scream. They whispered in his ears, urged him in his head. 'Go. Run!'; but he was trapped, trapped with these sounds. They whispered to him. 'Oh how worthless they all are.'

Why would they not leave him alone?

Solitude.

A cold and empty room. Cold. The feeling was tangible, like icy fingertips running over numb skin. The days were a blur of sleep cycles as night and day mixed into a mess of light and darkness. I had no idea how long I had been stuck in here for, my tally had failed long ago after I fell unconscious from hunger; now, I had no clue. Food came twice a week per week, drink came once per day. In here I was barely being kept alive. Under the rain and storms, water would drip in the corner for hours. Drip. Drip. That stupid forsaken drip that droned on and on; it echoed around my chamber. Sometimes mud would leak through the singular window of the back of the cell, filling my tiled cell with slushed soil. The cold would not go away, its icy embrace encased me, the cold, oh the cold.

A blade in a ballet.

He flourished, his control of the blade was majestic; the silver weapon twisted and span around his body; elegant like the soft autumn breeze but powerful like the raging whirlwind. His opponent stepped forward, a hand held behind his back, his blade held upright - splitting his face. They faced one another in silence, one hooded, the other in armour.

The hooded rushed forward, his blade extended. The armoured knocked the blade to the right and stepped to the left, spinning around his foe and hitting the hooded with the hilt of his blade. The hooded lurched forward, stopped, and dashed to the right. The armoured span to react, but he caught nothing but his afterimage. The dancing blade sparked as it skimmed across the Armoured's chest. He stepped back and placed two hands on his blade. The hooded stopped in front of him and smiled, his grip tightening on his blade. The armoured stepped, twisted his feet and span, his sword following his arc. The power of the swing blasted a shockwave forward, knocking the hooded off his feet. The hooded rolled to the right to dodge a downward stab, the unbreakable blade cracked the ground. The armoured ripped his silver blade out of the ground, swinging it limply to the right to keep the hooded zoned off.

He used this chance; the hooded once again darted forward, his blade sheathed. The hooded jumped onto the Armoured's chest, his fingers slipping between the kinks in the armour. He pulled and pulled, attempting to break apart the titan's armour. The armoured flailed magnificently, attempting to retain his balance whilst trying to rip him off. The hooded bounced off and out of the reach of his blade, a plate of armour in his hand.

A glimmer of white teeth shone through the shadows of his hood, giving out a sinister aura as he once again drew his sword. Their blades came together in wonderful sparks and metallic knolls that filled the air with the music of battle. Clashes moved at an inhuman speed, the power behind each of their attacks was overly destructive, each clash blasting shockwaves outwards. Neither would back down, neither let up. The courtyard their battle had taken place in was completely destroyed, the stone walls surrounding them nothing more than ruins; the green grasses overturned, the flowers flattened. The blades; the blades specifically made for these two masters, could not hold against their incredible power. They shattered; hundreds of shards of metal fell to the ground.

Neither had won, yet neither had fell. A duel of two true masters.

The crystal kingdom.

My shoes tapped against sapphire road as I looked up at the azure sky, my feet carried me towards the arena in which the event was being held. Ruby towers and ivory citadels looked down upon me as I walked in awe of the city I had lived in for so long. Looks... Can be deceiving. A phrase everybody had learned and known since childhood; the single greatest truth we had to teach to our own children.

This city was known across the world as the most beautiful, gazed on by the masses as a symbol of perfection, of utopia. That word, utopia, could not have been further from the truth. What people saw as perfection, I only saw as flawed, threatening. Those ivory towers were no comfort, offered no protection, they gazed down with certainty, with complete overbearing power. They confined us within, whilst smiling at the outside world.

I finally made it to the arena, and took my seat. The azure sky overhead was slowly turning pink as the rays of sunset cast themselves across the blue marble. In the centre of the arena, a young man kneeled before a soldier, the gun poised at his throat.

"This is for Ivora!" A simple bread thief, hungry and alone. His life was snuffed and his voice silenced. The best part? Nobody would ever know outside of this small town, they made sure that their reputation was never ruined, never tarnished. Looks can be deceiving, for even the most beautiful rose still has thorns.

From dusk to dawn.

In the earliest of the morning hours, before the birds woke the world with their singing, and the darkness befell the land; the wet sound of feet splashing through the rain echoed across the horizon. A black coat adorned his shoulders, black swollen gloves wrapped his hands and a knitted hat sat atop his head. The darkened sky above swirled with a subtle passion, the stars were shining with a vibrancy unseen to his eyes, the moon seemed almost… Powerful, as if it had an aura of life surrounding it. The light from the sun just reached over the horizon, clashing with the darkness above, slowly pushing it back as it broke into the field.

He stopped moving, catching his breath, headphone wires dangling from his ears. The world stopped, allowing him to throw all stress and pressure away and simply observe this distant battle in all its beauty. The gorgeous pink befitting the wonder that the horizon held in its grasp. He allowed his lips to tug upward, curving his expression into a joyous smile. The emerald grass that blew in the slight breeze beneath him shined as the light reflected off the morning dew, the sun finally rose past the horizon, staring directly at him. Dawn. He grinned, and made his way home.

She rested her head in her hand as she prepared for the long journey home, through dusk, no less. The light of the evening was a mix of orange and pink, a shade she had never seen before. Her eyes widened as she took in the gorgeous sight as the world reflected the incredible light back at her. Wispy clouds flicked and swirled above, coloured pink and red from the strange sunlight. It perked her up from her slipping consciousness and reinvigorated her. She spent the journey staring in awe at the wonderful scenery.

A beautiful scene to end the day, she thought. She threw her backpack on, and made her way home. Dusk, she smiled.

The blank canvas.

No sight had I witnessed before that was so tranquil, and so pearlescent; the world stretched out before me, every flower and every blade of grass, even the sky - a gleaming white. Bleak. Every step I took through the empty space left a footprint in the grass, leaving it verdant and vibrant. Colour pulsed from my fingertips to my toes with every piece of this empty painting I touched brought the life back into it. Colour flowed from me like water cascading down a mountain, into the sea of bleakness below. The small area I stood in was slowly regaining its energy, fuchsia flowers and emerald grass lit up with radiance.

What needed its colour back was the beautiful azure sky. It was a blank white, colourless and empty like the rest of the world. I wanted its azure beauty to illuminate the world once more. Perhaps it could restore colour to the void. I sat in my patch of moss green and ice blue staring out at the blank sky, a black sun watched over the world. Clouds slowly brushed across the scene like models on a set. The sound of a soft breeze did not follow them, their wispy cotton seemed hard and static.

No animals joined the scene, except for the insects I had brought into the land of colour. I moved my hands slowly, thinking about how I could recolour the sky, slowly lying on my back. I looked back down at my hand, of which I had just been laying on. My power did not only bring happiness, but also pain. Crimson blood leaked out of the small cut on my hand and dropped onto the grass, spreading through the blank canvas like a virus. Each drop of blood released a ruby red darkness, contaminating all that I had graced with my touch, and all that I had not. The bleak world was slowly becoming a hellish red that I had no chance of stopping. I plucked a single rose and held it to my chest, as I watched the sky turn scarlet, the black sun watched disapprovingly.

It was no longer a blank canvas.

Embers.

Like a firefly buzzing in the shadows of the moon, but silent like the wispy clouds floating on above; are the orange bulbs that spawn from a flickering flame. Tiny lanterns filled with powerful light floating away from the crackling fire, up; up; into the darkness, before they are snuffed by the cold of the night. There are always more to take their place as the blaze below spits out ember after ember. They were silent fireflies that drifted on the wind, a beauty only meant to disappear, only fated to have a brief existence. In the end, that only made them ever more beautiful; evanescent.

Once...

Once; the world was not ash, not grey, but vibrant and full of life. People roamed the streets with joy plastered across their faces, the skies were like sapphire and the sun illuminated everything with such radiance. What was once beautiful now remains scarred, and in ash, because such is the nature of man; to destroy. Man is jealous and envious, and destruction is his forte. He takes. So this wondrous city fell and with it; the world.

Scorches mark the ruins of buildings, and the red sun highlights the ashen snow that floats to my feet. The sky resembles the blood that drips from barbaric displays, and my drawn blade. It taints the grey snow my feet are planted in, colouring it, changing it. I see only my own hatred in that crimson. I wish for the beauty to return, for my joyous people to smile and cheer once more… I could have done no more to protect the world I loved and held so dearly, and so the feeling of helplessness and finally; loneliness, set in. The world is now cruel and cold - an awful wasteland that holds only sorrow and emptiness for those that venture into it. Unfortunately, I have found the one thing that can seal this hole in my heart, this yearn for the return of vibrancy. Revenge. I tilted my sword so that the red sun reflected off the shining silver.

Such empty tears.

Tears. They fell from his eyes and splashed on the pure white sheets of his bed. Why? He wasn't entirely sure. His mind raging and rambling, it was hard to form coherent thoughts, but words stuck in the forefront of his mind. Helpless, hopeless, failure. Like leeches on his mind they sucked and sapped all positivity. You'd think he was happy, his perfect little life with his perfect friends and everything he could ever ask for. It wasn't the materialism. It was his own mind. It wanted to destroy itself, every second it was left alone it chipped away at itself. Told itself that it was worthless. He smiled through the day, laughed in the calls with his friends, smiled through movies and books, but his mind attacked incessantly like a woodlouse making its way through bark it sunk in and stayed. The negativity he thought had long gone and ate away with insatiable hunger. The tears were empty, but her words were not. Her words cracked into his mind, tapped at its shell, and whispered. She whispered her beauty, her positivity shined through like rays of sunlight through a canopy of leaves.

Love, a strong emotion. It tugged at his mind, taking him further and further into the light, away from the snapping jaws of depression's unending starvation.

He lived for another, and through giving himself entirely, he found peace.

A rose in a blizzard.

A single rose that stood strong against the blizzard, a bombardment of ice, of death.
Nothing around him remained, the garden it fell from called for its return, but life didn't work that way. It wouldn't go down without a fight; however, and so in the eye of the storm it stood tall, its blood red petals illuminating the white wasteland.

The storm subsided, but the rose had not recovered. It started to wilt, the pain of its battle lingering on those crimson petals. A girl, wandering through the snowed lands, picked the rose, smiling sadly at its pain.

She took it home, nurtured it, cared for it, her pretty smile a radiant beam that healed the falling petals. The rose revived with renewed vigour.
She returned it to its rightful place in the green garden, and with the sun beating down upon its blood red petals, light returned to the garden, another rose returning to its rightful place, the place it belonged.

Interlinked.

Polar opposite and yet locked together, unable to leave one another, unable to break free. When one latches on to you the other is always there, and already waiting to pounce. The higher you climb the further you can fall; they are two sides of the same coin. Interlinked and always together; Joy and Sorrow. Interconnected within the bridges of our consciousness and yet they seem so separate. Joy is a cool calm anger waiting for its other half, the collected worrisome sadness to seep in, as once joy leaves, only sorrow can fill that void. You wish for joy in the expected absence of sorrow, you think that smiles only push away the veiled emotion, but it only brings it closer as it waits in the dark. The elation of joy, interlinked with the depression of sorrow. Such is the power of emotion.

Alone in death...

To reap is to harvest. To take what you have so meticulously built up from nothing. I am no reaper; I am a thief. I take the souls of the living that he has so thoughtlessly created, and send them into eternity, for better or for worse. For four millennia, I have witnessed lives end, unable to stop the pain and the suffering they feel, that I feel. Drifting across this bleak planet, collecting their innocent souls, heavy with the sin of their father, and sending them to his judgement. They deserve not the hammer of his evil, for his guilt is as heavy as theirs.

A machine.

A machine. What does it do? What was it built for? It cranks out product after product, keeping the populace happy, at the expense of one soul; the mind. It works and works, harder than the machine, and keeps creating idea after idea. It started as something that was simply for the mind's own pleasure, but they wanted more, the machine NEEDED more. It needed more fuel, craved the energy of the mind, crushed its soul in the hopes of extracting one more idea for its never ending rampage. Grinders squeezed every idea for all its worth, milked it for every drop of the populace's applause, whilst it secretly intimidated the mind into more. Always more. It always needed more.

This wonderful invention now pollutes the sky with its lust for fuel. The once proud mind slaves away behind the scene, churning out product after product that is just the same as the last, and yet the crowd screams with ecstasy and joy, feeding the machine their applause.

Nothing but a machine. A simple machine.

Wouldn't you rather?

A simple question really, wouldn't you rather? Wouldn't you rather be in a hot bath at home, relaxing to the most beautiful music? Wouldn't you rather be lying on the soft white beaches of the Caribbean? Or perhaps gambling in Las Vegas until the early hours of the morning? The terrible revelation is that there is always somewhere better to be. You can never be in your perfect place. A sad truth. Wouldn't you agree?

Through the eyes of a trinket.

A locket, given at the age of five. A sparkle in her eye and a smile upon her face, the first things I saw as I was passed from mother to daughter, parent to child. My eyes looked on from the seat I had on the base of her throat, hanging from a chain around her neck. I promised myself I would keep her safe, I would always be her locket, that held the only picture of her father inside. Her name? Charlie.

Nine years old, four years of sitting on her chest, being her watchful protector, her friend. She moved, away from her friends, the tears washed over my silver body. I only wanted to hold her, to tell her it would be okay, but alas all I could do was watch, from the seat on the base of her throat, as she waved goodbye to her friends, people I had known for four years. Of course, I was still with her, she still held me so dearly, and that was all that mattered to me. I still mattered to her.

Fifteen years old. I watched the stress of school take her, break her down. She held me tightly in one hand, asking me for help, begging me to save her. I could not help, instead I offered her my prayers, hoped that my thoughts would cross into her mind. She held onto me for support, and all I could do was sit on her chest, looking up at the wonderful girl I had stayed with her entire life.

Seventeen. Scared, oh so scared, as I watched through the windscreen, her hands on the steering wheel of a metal beast. She laughs above me, freedom filling her breaths as she takes her car out for a drive for the first time. Her nights are spent passionately with her new boyfriend, and I watch, feeling replaced, as he takes me from her neck and places me on the desk.

Twenty-three. A white dress and a veil covering her face. I can feel her pulse, her racing heartbeat loud and powerful. I can feel her disjointed breathing; she is more nervous than she has ever been in her life. I sit on her chest, as she walks down the aisle, her arm linked around her step-father's, before he passes her to the groom. He is the most important thing in her life now, the man standing before her. I'm the happiest I can ever be because I realise that she is the happiest she will ever be. She will never forget me.

Twenty-eight. After bearing through the screaming of my beloved Charlie; I feel my heart ache with love. A small new-born boy. Jet black hair like his father, and angelic baby blue eyes. She holds him close to her chest and whispers in his ear; 'Welcome to the world, Arthur.' Arthur, the name of her father, who's face is contained within me, in her locket.

Forty. Arthur is twelve years old, healthy, and as handsome as his father. I'm so proud of her, the work she does, the boy she has raised. My darling Charlie. I still sit on her chest, as she works as hard as she ever has, living comfortably and happily with her family. She never forgets to put me on, not once in thirty-five years. All I wish is that the man inside me, her father, could see the woman she had become.

Fifty-three. A grandmother to Arthur's first child. She's almost as happy as she was on the day of her wedding. I watch like a proud parent, or more like a great grandparent, from my seat on the base of her throat as she holds her granddaughter for the first time. She cries and squeals, before looking up into Charlie's loving eyes, and calming. That's my girl, I thought, as her smiles and giggles reached the ears of the new-born child.

Life flew by. I watched her from the age of five grow into a fine young woman, with a beautiful and loving family, and a job she loved. Her son gave her a granddaughter that she cherished her time with, but such happiness cannot last forever.

Seventy-Five. The death of her husband. The cause of this misfortune was cancer, something that had given Charlie and her dear husband more than enough time to complete their bucket list. I dangled from her hand and watched through the crystal raindrops falling from above as his coffin was lowered into the ground. She held me tightly to her chest as she had a hundred times before, but this time felt different. She wasn't asking me for comfort, but simply to remember. To hold her memories for her. I promised, even though she could never hear me, that I would do exactly that.

It was a short five years after that, that I watched my dearest Charlie die peacefully, surrounded by her family. Her entire life she had held me close, and in her last moments, I saw her contemplate whether to pass me down as her mother had down to her. She opened the locket, and saw the picture of her father inside. A salty tear rolled down her cheek, before pulling me to her chest, to her heart, to hear it slowly come to a halt. Still.

I would stay with her to the end of time. Through eternity and back. I had nowhere else to be, but by her side. And so I remain here, in the coffin of my former owner. My dearest Charlie. Her cold bone fingers curled around my chain.

The northern lights.

Twinkling stars were stuck on the blanket that wrapped around the world, the only light in the darkness of the land. The white snow reflected what it could, but slowly and surely the light was taken by the shadows. Everything fell silent, and the world felt empty; colour. Colour burst into the darkness as the northern lights floated across the sky, twisting and turning like lines of verdant and violet silk slithering across the blanket of stars above. Colour lit up the reflective snow below, bouncing the beautiful light off into the bleakness of the void above. From the eyes on the ground it was truly pulchritudinous, a taker of breath, a rare precious scene drifting beneath the stars. If only it lasted. Sadly, the lights and their colour were evanescent; fleeting.

Doves.

White as the most luminous pearl, their feathers soft and silky to the touch. These doves covered the cobbled ground like the verdant grass outside the arena, a sea of white twitching heads and black beady eyes. It was this view to which she walked into the silent ruins of the old coliseum, her father's great sword dragging slowly behind her. She took a few steps forward, breathed in deeply, and swung the massive beast with all her might, both hands on the grip. The doves ahead fluttered away, running from the danger, landing only a couple of meters further away. She used her momentum to throw her weight forward, dragging the great sword from the cobbled ground and into the air. The sky above filled with the flitter of these radiant white beauties. She continued to walk, the doves parting for her as she dragged the huge weapon behind her. In the centre of the coliseum, the light shined into the coliseum from above, providing sunlight for a single flower that grew in-between the stones, searching for its light.

She fell to her knees and brushed her cheek against its soft petals. She lay the great sword next to the flower, and pressed her hands together.

"My prayers, father. For the greatest gladiator, who was never given the opportunity to enter the arena. I will follow your legacy." She bowed her head, allowed the few tears she had to fall, and stood. She turned and exited, leaving the great sword jammed in-between the stones, behind the flower. The light poured into the coliseum behind her, and reflected wonderfully off of the old blade.

Shriek.

A blood curling scream drifted through the air as the hunter's scythe left a harrowing hole in the wraith's torso. He fixed his hat and flourished his trench coat. His boots were wet from the moisture of the soil as he made his way through darkened woods. An old town, cloaked in mist, revealed itself to the hunter as he broke the treeline. Shouts and screams floated around the town as if the mist itself was in agony. He drew his scythe once again from his back, and spun it in one hand as he stepped into the streets. He passed a heavy iron gate that remained wide open, welcoming the dark forces that hid beyond.

Wraiths roamed freely, drifting over the bodies of their - now - dead victims. They seemed hollow, a floating cloak with nothing but bleak emptiness in the sleeves and under the hood. The hunter pulled the hat down over his eyes, held a lantern in one hand, and pressed onward. The wraiths whispered in the shadows, their hoarse voices dancing across the shadows, yet the town felt eerily empty. A scream. Closer, and closer it came. It was charging like an angered bull. The hunter ducked under the swipe of one of the wraiths that attempted to remove his cranium from his body. His coat fluttered behind him, windswept across the ground. The hunter stood, lashed his scythe out and felt the cold steel grab the wraiths neck. With all his strength he pulled against the spirit's momentum, severing the head of the creature from its body. The hunter stood and dusted himself down, clipping the lantern to his belt. He fingered his scythe, feeling for marks or imperfections. A dark, smoke like aura surrounded the deceased wraith's ethereal body. The hunter lifted the scythe onto his shoulder and pushed onward.

He stopped at the cathedral, its stone structure loomed overhead. He knew his prey awaited him inside, and so swallowed his fear and steeled his resolve. He opened the two huge wooden doors and bathed in the dark hue of moonlight that shone through the single circular window above. The hunter walked through the silent halls, and stepped up to the altar. His gloved hands, encased in leather, brushed against ancient engravings. Dust collected upon his fingertips.

Without warning, the doors behind him slammed shut, allowing a gust of air to blow out his lantern and cause the tail of his worn and ragged coat to flutter. The light that sprinkled through the doorway had retreated. Across window above, that allowed a spotlight of beautiful azure light to sprinkle in through the circular view. All light blotted out for a moment as a creature skittered across the window. Cold silence drifted through the room.

The window smashed and the majestic creature landed softly, barely making a sound. The light disappeared entirely, the hunter scrambled for a match, dropping the match box in the process. Silently he fell to his knees and used his hands as minesweepers, finally grabbing it and lighting his lantern. He held it up as he stood, only to stare into the creature's empty, black, eyes. It snarled at him, before bringing its great claw into the air and slamming it into the hunter with enough force to send him smashing into the opposite wall. Broken and bruised, the hunter pulled himself to his feet. The lantern was still in his hand, the scythe, his back. He clipped the lantern to his hip once again, and felt the leather of his gloves as they stretched and scratched whilst he tightened his two handed grasp on his - now - drawn scythe, his grip on the weapon was talon like.

The soft silence clawed at the edges of the flickering flame that flittered at his hip. The creature broke the silence with a blood curling shriek, the hunter dived and rolled under the swipe, spinning the reaper in his hands as he came up, slicing at the underbelly of the beast. Blood splattered over the parish floors a luminous orange. The creature was now traceable as the luminous blood dripped from the open wound. The hunter pursued for a follow up attack, of which he only managed to glance its back legs; more luminous brazen liquid trickled down the beast.

The beast moved like no other creature he had hunted before. Like a wraith; it moved with an odd spirit-like sway to it, each step felt calculated, light. Like a dancer it moved with elegance, it was with that movement, plus the luminous blood, that the hunter realised what the creature he was hunting truly was.

A Ghoul. Ghouls were rare, and dangerous, but this one was special. From the wispy movement to its heightened aggression, it was noticed that the Ghoul possessed the soul of a wraith. A powerful wraith. The hunter, now aware of his enemy, moved quickly. He unclipped the lantern from his hip and threw it at where he thought the circular window was, for he knew the Ghoul had somehow blocked the light to turn the battle in his favour. The lantern smashed, and surely enough it set the cloak covering the spotlight ablaze. The hunter weaved in-between two more strikes, before the dark blue hue returned to the chamber, and the spotlight gave full view of the Ghoul's horrific form. Its teeth were sharpened to a point, its eyes the blackest beads – far too small for its giant head, adding to the abomination. Its body, were it to stand, was large enough to touch the high ceiling of the parish. It adorned a ghost like ragged cloth around its neck that flittered in the draft. Noticing the light, the hunched creature only moved faster, determined to end the hunter's life. It was no use with the light on his side, he ducked, hooked his scythe around the creature's neck, and pulled down like a guillotine. The Ghoul's shrieking head made a 'thud' sound as it cracked against the floor, and rolled to a stop. Its black beady eyes grew dull with every passing moment…

Paradise, Sunset and Nothingness.

Light that fills the landscape with beauty, that warms the heart of all that enter its gates. Its beauty blinds all.

The brazen orange of a beautiful sunset that sinks into the bluest of oceans, at the edge of the world.

A bleak void, empty of all. Tranquil, peaceful, without a sound, and strangely pulchritudinous. Unforgettable.

So beautiful is one's imagination.

THE END

Made in the USA
Charleston, SC
26 April 2016